Shakespeare Tales

A Midsummer Night's Dream

First published 2016 by

Bloomsbury Education, an imprint of Bloomsbury Publishing Plc
50 Bedford Square, London, WC1B 3DP

www.bloomsbury.com

Bloomsbury is a registered trademark of Bloomsbury Publishing Plc
Text copyright © Terry Deary 2016
Illustrations © Tambe 2016

A CIP catalogue for this book is available from the British Library

ISBN: 978-1-4729-1777-5 (paperback)

Printed and Bound by CPI Group (UK) Ltd, Croydon CR0 4YY

1 3 5 7 9 10 8 6 4 2

MIX
Paper from
responsible sources
FSC® C020471
www.fsc.org

TERRY DEARY

Shakespeare Tales

A Midsummer
Night's Dream

Illustrated by

Tambe

BLOOMSBURY EDUCATION
AN IMPRINT OF BLOOMSBURY

LONDON OXFORD NEW YORK NEW DELHI SYDNEY

Contents

Act 1

Athens and arguments

The servant's tale

R ichard Armin was a Fool. No, no, no. I don't mean he was a buffoon or a blockhead, a dunce or a dog-heart, a beef-wit or a bird-brain.

I mean he was a jester, a comic, a wit. Master Shakespeare, the great play writer, hired Armin to play the part of the Fool in all of his plays. Even in the sad plays Master Shakespeare had to write a scene or two for a clown. That's what so many people came to the theatres to see.

Master Shakespeare wrote a terribly sad play called 'Hamlet' where a prince set out to avenge his father's murder. By the end of the play there were ten bodies, like litter, on the stage. Prince Hamlet himself died. But even that sad play had to have a part for Richard Armin to play a buffoon... Armin acted as a gravedigger who made jokes about skeletons and skulls as he dug. A young girl died and Armin made the crowds laugh. I cried.

Oh how those audiences loved him. The laughed and cheered and thought he was a wonder of the world. There was one person who loved Richard Armin the most, though, more than the sun and the moon and the stars. That person was Richard Armin. Yes, Armin the Fool loved himself like a cat loves fish, like a hawk loves rabbits and like our donkey, Dolly, loves oats.

When he stepped off the stage, Richard Armin was a bully and a boaster. I was his servant and I never saw the funny man smile. No one liked him, but Master Shakespeare had to keep him in the acting company because the crowds loved him and paid their pennies to watch a Fool act the fool.

No one else had a servant. Not even Mr Shakespeare himself. But my father had sold me to a farmer to work in the stables, milk the cows, feed the pigs, plant the cabbages and take the chickens to market. One summer that foul and filthy farmer beat dear Dolly the donkey so I decided to run away with her to Warwick.

Dolly ate grass by the roadside. But I couldn't eat grass and I almost starved to death. That was when I met a company of travelling actors, led by Mr Shakespeare. They took me in and fed me. Dolly and I helped them travel from town to town. She pulled their carts and carried their costumes while I helped with the cooking and cleaning and mending. They paid me with dinners. It was a joy, a dream. A midsummer dream. I loved my life with them.

But it was Clown Armin who made me his special slave. 'I am the most popular man in the theatre company, girl, young

Molly,' he used to say. 'I shine more than the rest, like a bright star. I am a star, girl, a star.' He struck me with a stick if I was slow to serve his wine or food. I hated him.

It was when the company played Master Shakespeare's 'A Midsummer Night's Dream' that I finally hit back.

But let me tell you about the play first...

The play

**Athens, Greece. Long, long ago.
The palace of Duke Theseus**

It's his wedding day in four days' time. Theseus should be happy. He should be excited. He should be jumping up and down crying, 'I'm so happy I could kiss a crocodile.'

But he's worried. Will the wedding be boring? He tells his servant that the young people of Athens must add to the excitement. **'Stir up the Athenian youth to merriments,'** he orders.

Before the wedding day Theseus still has to work. He must settle and fettle the problems of the people of Athens. He's their Duke, that's his job. This particular morning he has to hear a moaning man called Egeus. What's wrong with old Egeus? It's his daughter, Hermia. What an annoying girl, Egeus wails.

Egeus says he wants the young woman to marry Demetrius. He is *such* lovely young man, Egeus says. But Hermia refuses. She *re-fus-es*. Says she's in love with another young man called Lysander.

Egeus says Lysander has used witchcraft on Hermia to make her fall in love with him. 'This man has bewitched the heart of my child. He's come to her window and sung songs; he's given her gifts – bracelets made of his hair, rings, flowers and sweetmeats.'

Egeus knows the law of Athens. He wants Duke Theseus to let him carry out the law; 'Hermia must be *forced* to marry the lovely Demetrius... or be put to death... or send her away to live the rest of her days as a nun,' Egeus rages. 'Put. To. Death.'

Duke Theseus decides. 'Hermia,' he says, 'Your father should be like a god. Demetrius is a fine gentleman.'

Hermia snaps back, 'So is Lysander.'

'But your father does not want him to marry you.'

The bold girl argues on. 'Then my father should look at Lysander through my eyes. Tell me, what is the worst that will happen,

if I refuse to wed Demetrius?' she says.

Theseus is stern and angry. 'Die or live the rest of your days as a nun, shut away from all men.'

She shrugs. 'Then I'll live and die a nun.'

Theseus says he is getting married at the next new moon in four nights' time. He gives Hermia four days to think about it... and maybe change her mind.

Demetrius has also come along to the Duke's court. He begs Hermia to marry him. Lysander is there too. He says that if old Egeus likes Demetrius so much maybe Demetrius should marry Egeus.

Lysander has lost but he won't give up. **'The course of true love never did run smooth,'** he tells Hermia.

Hermia's friend, Helena, can't believe the mess Hermia is in. 'If I were you I'd marry Demetrius. He is my perfect man. I wish *I* could marry him,' she says.

Hermia tells her friend her greatest secret. 'Tomorrow night Lysander and I are

running away from Athens. We're meeting in the woods. You can *have* Demetrius. He's yours. Take him. And good luck to you.'

But Helena is feeling spiteful. She mutters to herself, 'Demetrius used to love me before he saw Hermia. If I tell him about Hermia's plan to run off with Lysander then he'll be oh so grateful to me. I'll spoil Hermia's little dreams and schemes. Just you see.'

Oh dear. Oh dear, oh dear. Oh dear, oh dear, oh dear.

A house in Athens

Meanwhile, there is another meeting planned in the woods near Athens tomorrow night. A group of workmen. Duke Theseus wants fun and games at his wedding? The workmen want to please him so they will put on a play.

The men are Snug the joiner, Flute the bellows-mender, Snout the tinker, and Starveling the tailor. But the bossiest and barmiest of them all is Bottom the weaver.

Not one of them is an actor. But they each think acting is easy.

Will they get mixed up with Hermia and Lysander's plan to run away? Of course they will!

Fights and fairies

The servant's tale

Master Richard Armin the clown didn't like me. Oh, he liked having a servant. It made him look better than the other actors. It made him feel important. But he didn't like me. And he really hated my donkey, Dolly. She was the best donkey in the world. She pulled one of the company carts through muddied lanes and rutted roads.

She never seemed to grow tired. But Master Armin didn't like her.

'She smells,' he said.

'No she doesn't,' I argued.

He shrugged. 'You wouldn't notice. You sleep with the beast so you smell just as bad. And she makes that awful braying noise.'

'Not as awful as the braying noise you make in the roadside taverns when you start to boast,' I thought. I didn't say it, though.

'I heard your donkey bellow when we were in the middle of a play the other day,' the company clown said. 'Our new play needs the head of a donkey,' he hissed. 'I have to wear it. I have a clumsy wooden one. I may just cut off your donkey's head to make a better mask.'

Oh, how he laughed at his joke. I thought he would choke with laughing. The awful thing was that it was true

about the head of an ass being part
of Master Shakespeare's new play. Armin
wouldn't really cut off Dolly's head.
Would he?

The play

A wood near Athens

It's evening and the runaway lovers, Hermia and Lysander, are heading for the woods to meet and escape from Egeus.

The workmen are making their way to the woods to practise their play.

What they don't know is that there is a group of magical spirits already living in the woods. They are the fairies. They are the Fairy King, Oberon, the Fairy Queen, Titania, and their elf-servants, led by mischief-maker, Puck.

Now you may think fairies are happy creatures. But not the ones who live in the woods of Athens. These fairies quarrel and argue and squabble and fight just like humans.

This particular fight is so fierce even the elves hide in acorn cups from fear. What are they fighting about? A serving boy, stolen from an Indian king. He is Titania's servant. Oberon wants the boy for himself.

'All I want is the little boy,' the Fairy King sighs.

'You couldn't buy him for all of Fairyland,' Titania sneers. 'I promised his mother I'd take care of him.'

Oberon is getting angry. 'How long are you planning to stay in this wood?'

he asks.

'Till after I see Theseus married,' the Fairy Queen tells him

'Give me the boy and I'll come with you,' Oberon says.

'No,' she says and floats away with her fairies.

He shouts after her, angrily, 'Before you leave this wood I'll have my revenge. You wait and see.'

Oh dear. Oberon wants revenge on Titania because she won't give him her serving boy. Helena wants revenge on Hermia because Demetrius is in love with Hermia not Helena. Lysander wants revenge on Demetrius because Demetrius is insisting that Hermia marries him not Lysander. What a tangle!

Oberon, the Fairy King, makes a plan to get his revenge. He orders his wicked servant, Puck, to find a magical flower. If Puck drips the juices of the flower on someone's eyes then he or she will fall in love with the first person they see.

Oberon tells Puck his plan. 'When we have the juice of the flower, we'll drop some on Titania's eyes while she's asleep. She'll fall madly in love with something in the woods... a lion, a bear, or wolf, or a bull, a meddling monkey, or busy ape. I can cure her by giving her the juice of another plant – but I won't do that till she gives me the little boy as my page.'

Puck flies off to find the flower and
Oberon waits in the woods. He sees
Demetrius walk by, followed by Helena.
She wants him, remember, but he
wants Hermia. Demetrius shouts and rages
at her, 'Stop following me. I don't love you
and I never will. Leave me alone. It makes

me sick to look at you. Now go. I need to find Hermia and Lysander and stop them running off together.'

He storms off and leaves Helena alone in the gloomy woods. That's when Oberon decides to help her. Puck returns with the magical flower juice and the King of the Fairies tells him to put some of the juice in the Demetrius's eyes so he will fall in love with Helena.

Oberon explains, 'You'll know the man I mean because he is dressed in clothes from Athens.' (That was a silly thing to say... as you will soon see.) Then the King takes the rest of the flower juice and goes off to play his trick on Titania.

He finds his Queen and drops the juice on her eyelids. She'll fall in love with the first thing she sees.

In another part of the wood, Puck finds the young man dressed in clothes from Athens. 'Ah!' he thinks. 'This must be the man Oberon meant.'

Of course it isn't. It's Lysander. (I told you Oberon was silly, didn't I?) Lysander is having a small sleep before he runs away with Hermia. Puck drips the magic flower juice in his eyes.

Helena is still wandering through the woods, remember. She finds Lysander sleeping and he wakes up. Who is the first person he sees? Helena, of course.

He rushes after her, telling her how

much he loves her – the magic flower juice has done its work. She flees. Lysander must be mad, she thinks.

Hermia is sleeping nearby and wakes from a nightmare. She is alone. Where is her love Lysander? She rushes off to find him.

What. A. Mess. And it is all about to get worse.

Juices and jokes

The servant's tale

That day we were playing in a city called Nottingham. We had set up in the town square on market day and hundreds of people had gathered to watch Master Shakespeare's play, 'A Midsummer Night's Dream'.

There were lots of vegetables for sale in the market and Master Shakespeare was worried. 'If they don't like my play they may take the most rotten, slimy and stinking vegetables and throw them at me,' he said.

But the Nottingham crowds loved the play. The three stories were a tangle. Hermia loved Lysander, but the magic flower juice made Lysander love Helena. Helena loved Demetrius but Demetrius wanted to marry Hermia.

The King of the Fairies was at war with his wife. In the same woods the workmen of Athens were practising their play. Master Richard Armin was chief clown in the company and this was his biggest scene. The one where he played a stupid weaver called Bottom and made everyone laugh. Oh how he loved that scene. Oh how he loved himself.

Nottingham was the day when it all went wrong.

The play

A wood near Athens

Bossy Bottom leads the workers. He is a star, he thinks. He will change the words of the play to make it better.

But Bottom has bad luck. As he begins to play his part the mischief spirit Puck comes along. With all his magic powers he changes Bottom's head so it looks like the head of a donkey – an ass's head for a man with the brain of a donkey.

His friends, the workers, see the monstrous head and they flee into the woods. Wouldn't you? **'O monstrous! O strange! We are haunted,'** they cry.

But Bottom doesn't know that his head looks like a donkey's. He is left alone. 'They've run away? It's just some joke to scare me,' he says.

He wanders into a grassy clearing in the woods where Titania is lying asleep. Her avenging husband, Oberon, has smeared her eyes with the juice of the magic flower. She will fall in love with the first thing she sees.

When Bottom comes along she wakes up. She sees the weaver with a donkey's head and, of course, she falls in love with him. Oberon's cruel joke just got better.

Titania orders her fairies to take Bottom to her palace and care for him. **'Feed him with apricots and dewberries, with purple grapes, green figs, and mulberries,'** she sighs.

The servant's tale

My donkey, Dolly, caused all the trouble in Nottingham market place. The actors were playing on a platform in the middle of the market. Dolly had been behind the stage. But she could smell the cabbages and the corn, the turnips and the carrots. Most of all the carrots. I had tied her up but I was careless. The rope had come loose and Dolly started to follow her nose towards the carrots, trailing the rope behind her.

First she pushed her way through the crowds as Master Richard Armin was playing the part of Bottom with his ass's head. Someone grabbed her rope but she just dragged the man along the cobbles, kicking and biting anyone who tried to stop her. She started to bray.

No one was watching Mr Armin any
more. When Dolly brayed a woman even
shouted, 'She makes a better ass than you
do, Bottom.'

I couldn't see Mr Armin's face under the ass mask but his fists were tight and white with fury. I knew that Dolly was in trouble.

Dolly snatched a mouthful of carrots and allowed me to lead her back behind the stage. I tied her tight to the frame of the stage this time. That way she couldn't cause any more trouble, I thought. I was wrong.

The crowd had loved the escaping donkey. Even Mr Shakespeare was wiping tears of laughter from his eyes.

But I knew one man would be crying tears of rage. One very dangerous man.

The play

Another part of the wood

The four lovers from Athens are wandering around in the wood. Oberon watches as Hermia and Demetrius argue. He realises that Puck has made a mistake. Oberon cries, 'This is the woman; but this is not the man.'

Hermia is seeking her true love, Lysander, and rushes off.

Demetrius falls asleep. Oberon paints his eyelids with the magic flower juice. 'This is the man,' he tells Puck.

Demetrius awakes with the magic flower juice on his eyes and the first person he sees is not Hermia but Helena. She is being chased by Lysander who also has also fallen in love with her because if the love-juice. Yesterday they both loved Hermia. Today they both love Helena.

She is sure they are making fun of her and she is so, so angry. Outraged, she screams, "O spite! O hell! I see you are all trying to make fun of me.'

Puck is sent to sort out the lovers with the other juice. He paints it on Lysander's eyes.

Now Lysander will love Hermia and Hermia will love Lysander. That's good.

Helena will love Demetrius and Demetrius will love Helena. Phew!

Donkeys and dreams

The servant's tale

Master Richard Armin still had his part to play. He would be on the stage for another half an hour. Then he would come looking for me and Dolly the Donkey. He would be carrying his axe to cut off Dolly's head. She had made such a fool of him.

I crept around the market stalls and gathered the food that had fallen to the cobbles. Cabbages and carrots for Dolly, apples and cheese and bread for me.

We would run away together – just like the people in Master Shakespeare's play – we would hide in the forest. They said there was a forest called Sherwood near to Nottingham. One of the actors had told me Robin Hood lived there with his Merry Men and Maid Marion. Maybe they'd have room for one more – Maid Molly.

The play was going on and I had to get away...

The play

Titania's home

Oh how the Fairy Queen loves the man with the ass's head. She loves to kiss his floppy ears and cuddle him.

How Bottom loves to eat hay and oats.

They fall asleep together and Oberon tells Puck that they will release Titania from the spell. She has promised to give him the serving boy. Bottom gets his own head back and Titania wakes up.

'My Oberon!' she cries. 'What a midsummer night's dream I have dreamed. I thought I fell in love with an ass!'

Oberon and Titania are friends again and the Fairy King promises that both pairs of lovers – Helena and Demetrius, Hermia and Lysander – will be married on the same day as Theseus.

Of course old Egeus is still angry, but Demetrius no longer wants to marry his daughter so he has to let Lysander marry her instead. They all return to Athens, except for Bottom the Weaver who wakes up in the forest, puzzled by the strange dream he has had.

He stumbles back to the village and his friends are filled with joy to see him. If they perform their play for the three couples at the wedding then they will all be made rich by Duke Theseus.

The servant's tale

The play was hurrying to its end. I had tied Dolly to the steps that led up to the stage. I saw Master Armin stride across to leave the stage as Bottom finished his scene. His red eyes were full of hate and he reached for the knife on his belt.

I tugged at Dolly's rope but the knot was too tight. She felt my panic and jumped back. The rope pulled at the wood that held the steps and as Master Armin stood on the top step they crashed down, taking the clown with them.

The watching people of Nottingham roared with laughter. Master Armin picked himself up from the splintered steps and bared his yellow teeth at us as I fled with Dolly. I'd never be able to go back to Master Shakespeare's theatre company again.

We trotted to Sherwood Forest to hide till the company had left the city. We got there as darkness fell and found ourselves alone.

Workers and weddings

The servant's tale

Sherwood Forest was not full of outlaws with arrows and men in cosy caves. It was dark and damp and filled with spiders and ants, angry foxes and running rabbits that scared me when they scuttled though the summer-dry twigs.

My food soon ran out and the berries I found on the bushes made me sick. Even Dolly was unhappy, with no grass growing in the dead leaves between the trees.

I tried to sleep that night but every owl-hoot wakened me and scuttling mice raced over me to hide from the owl's clutching claws. When I did sleep a little I had a midsummer nightmare of Richard Armin sitting at a feast. When the silver cover was taken off the large serving dish I saw Dolly's unhappy head sitting there.

In the darkest hours a summer storm crashed through the trees and soaked me. There would be no happy ending for me like the one in Mr Shakespeare's tale.

I knew I'd die in Sherwood Forest. As the sky grew light I just wanted to get Dolly back to the road through the woods so someone would find her and care for her.

Poor Dolly didn't deserve to die... even if her carrot-hunting habit had led us here.

The play

The hour of Theseus' wedding

Duke Theseus has heard all about the play that Bottom and the workers have planned for the weddings.

He is happy to let them perform. **'I will hear that play,'** he says.

The workmen's play is muddled and mad as the workmen mumble and mix their words. The bride of Duke Theseus, Hippolyta, says, **'This is the silliest stuff that ever I heard.'**

But Theseus is kinder. 'These poor men

think they are great actors. If they believe that then so can we.'

The play ends with a dance and the workers are rewarded. Midnight strikes and the married couples make their way home.

As they go the invisible fairies bless the weddings. Puck looks down and says farewell. 'Now the hungry lion roars and the wolf howls at the moon.

The farmer snores, worn out from his work. The burned logs glow in the fireplace, and the owl's hoot makes sick people think about their own deaths. Now is the time of night when graves open wide and let out spirits to glide over the graveyard paths.'

Oberon and Titania, Puck and the fairies melt into the midsummer midnight air and vanish as if it has all been a dream... which maybe it is.

The servant's tale

I tumbled through the trees and found the road. The rainstorm had left it thick with mud and I plodded through puddles over my ankles. Then I heard shouting. 'Push harder, you idle layabouts. Push harder.'

I splashed along the road and saw the theatre company and their carts struggling through the swampy path and Master Armin shouting at the other actors. Master Armin was already angry with me. Now his face was purple with rage. Maybe the dream of him eating Dolly's head would come true. I turned to tiptoe away – if you can tiptoe through pools of muddy water.

Then a voice called, 'Molly... Molly! There you are!'

It was Master Shakespeare. He paddled along the road with a grin on his face.

'We are so glad to see you. And your beautiful donkey.'

'You are?'

'Of course. No one else can get us out of this swampy road. Come and help,' he pleaded.

'Master Armin will kill me,' I squeaked.

Master Shakespeare laughed. 'Master Armin will learn what all the other actors already know. We need you, Molly.'

'But...' I began.

'I know he's been an unkind master. He does not deserve you or Dolly. If I promise to make you MY servant, will you come back to join us? I'll pay you well and see that you eat like a lady.'

His smile was so gentle he melted my heart as if I had magic flower juice dripped on it.

'I will,' I said.

And so my midsummer night's nightmare ended and – like Hermia and Lysander, Theseus and Hippolyta, Helena and Demetrius – we all lived happily ever after.

All stories should end that way.

Did you know?

Shakespeare tells a tangled tale of mix-ups and magic. It shows us what happens when we turn silly! Shakespeare makes his characters ...

• **jealous** – like Helena who wants Demetrius

• **greedy** – like Fairy King Oberon who wants Queen Titania's serving boy

• **wicked** – like Puck who loves playing tricks on people for spite

• **bossy** – like Egeus who wants his daughter to marry the man HE has chosen

- **big-headed** – like Bottom the weaver who thinks he is a wonderful actor.

Of course Bottom ends up with a REALLY big head when Puck gives him the head of a donkey.

It's fun to see what happens when Shakespeare takes these characters and stirs them up in a story where magic makes anything possible.

Shakespeare was not just clever at making characters and stories. He was also wonderful with words.

Did you know that he used 17,677 different words in his work? And that of those words, Shakespeare invented an incredible 1,700 of them? He gave us many words that we use today. Here are just a dozen ...

1. Cold-blooded
2. Eyeball
3. Ladybird
4. Manager (in 'A Midsummer Night's Dream')
5. Scuffle
6. Bandit
7. Bedroom
8. Moonbeam
9. Gloomy
10. Gossip
11. Elbow
12. Dawn

Shakespeare also came up with some brilliant ways to insult people. Some of his words don't MEAN much to us these days but they sound wonderful when you say them out loud. Try these...

- moldwarp
- measle
- hedge-pig
- giglet
- puking

Then Shakespeare put his wonderful words together to make...

Thou leathern-jerkin, crystal-button, knot pated, agatering, puke stocking, caddis garter, smooth tongue, Spanish pouch!

What next?

You can enjoy Shakespeare's words. Try this with a friend and see who can come up with the nastiest insult. Take one Shakespeare word from list one, another from list 2 and another from list 3. Mix them any way you want then say them as if you really hate your partner... even though you don't!

List 1	List 2	List 3
bootless	plume-plucked	clack-dish
craven	fen-sucked	malt-worm
droning	knotty-pated	foot-licker
gleeking	dog-hearted	nut-hook
lumpish	toad-spotted	clotpole
mewling	sheep-biting	puttock
reeky	flap-mouthed	pumpion
weedy	swag-bellied	boar-pig
rank	boil-brained	ratsbane
pribbling	onion-eyed	maggot-pie

Have fun. Enjoy the taste of Shakespeare's words in your mouth.